Good Luck Bear

Good Luck Bear

by Greg Foley

SCHOLASTIC INC.

For those who find luck in the unexpected

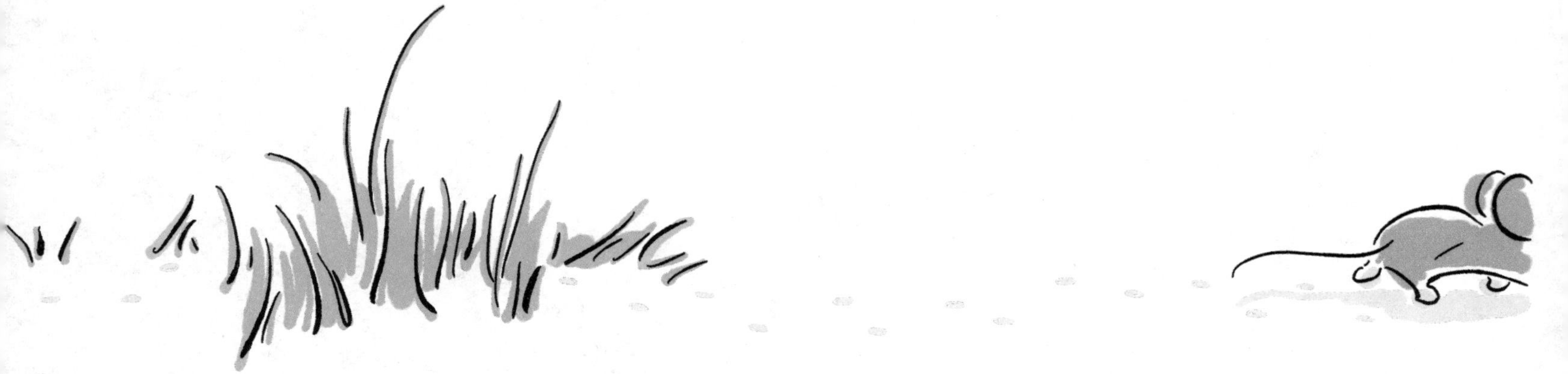

One day while lying in the grass,
a little bear found a clover
with three tiny leaves.

He showed it to his friend Mouse.
Mouse said, "If you find one
with four leaves,
it means that you're lucky."

Bear started looking for
a four-leaf clover.

Monkey saw him looking and said, "There is no such thing."

Turtle saw him looking and said, "That's going to take forever."

Elephant saw him and said,
"I remember seeing one,
but I forget where."

So Bear kept looking.

Groundhog asked,
"If you don't find one, does it mean
that you're unlucky?"

Squirrel came and said,
"I prefer them with three leaves."
And he took as many
as he could carry.

Then Bunny said, "Here's one!"
And he ate it.
"Good luck, Bear," he said.

The little bear felt
very unlucky.

Until he saw Mouse.
Mouse said, "I think I've found
something for you."

Bear went over to look.
"Does it have four leaves?"
he asked.

Mouse said, "No...

"...it has five!"

ISBN 978-0-545-84920-3

12 11 10 9 8 7 6 5 4 3 2   15 16 17 18 19 20/0

Printed in the U.S.A.   40

First Scholastic printing, January 2015

Set in American Typewriter Regular